Shoe Boxes

Written by Janet Berry, Kathy Havens,
Joetta Beaver, and Cheri Slinger
Illustrated by Jeremy Tugeau

PEARSON

Mandy and her brother and sister got new shoes. Her brother got a pair of shoes for his soccer game. The shoes came in a red box with white stripes on it.

Mandy's brother took the shoe box
home. He put a caterpillar in it. The
caterpillar liked his new home.

Mandy's sister got new baseball shoes
for her baseball game. The shoes came
in a blue box with a string.

Her sister took the shoe box and the string home. She put her baseball cards and the string in her shoe box.

Mandy got a new pair of blue shoes
for her birthday. Her shoes came in a
green box with flowers on it.

Mandy gave her shoe box to her baby sister. She sat on it. Oh, no!